WILBUR'S SPACE MACHINE

written and illustrated by
LORNA BALIAN

Holiday House/New York

Library of Congress Cataloging-in-Publication Data

Balian, Lorna.
Wilbur's space machine / written and illustrated
by Lorna Balian.—1st ed.
p.   cm.
Summary: Violet and Wilbur love the peace and quiet
of their valley and find the need for more space
when it is invaded by many neighbors,
including the obstreperous Googie.
ISBN 0-8234-0836-1
[1. Neighborliness—Fiction.]   I. Title.
PZ7.B1978W1   1990
[E]—dc20   90-55095   CIP   AC
ISBN 0-8234-0836-1

For Jed and Noah, with love

Violet and Wilbur lived all by themselves
smack in the middle of nowhere.
They lived simply, in clean, peaceful space,
and they were happy with their lives.

In spring,
they planted their garden.

During the summer,
they tended their plants.

When autumn came,
they stored their harvest.

And all through the winter,
they read books and slept.

But gradually—
so gradually Violet and Wilbur hardly noticed—

other people moved into their valley.
A family here, a family there, until . . .

they were surrounded by a whole crowded village. There were people, pets, houses, stores, factories, roads, bicycles, motorcycles, buses, and trucks. There was smoke, smog, trash, garbage— and there was Googie.

"Our lovely valley is polluted," said Wilbur sadly.
"We don't have clean, peaceful space anymore."
"No, dear, but we have each other," said Violet.
"We have each other
AND we have Googie!" said Wilbur,
scowling at the boy who lived next door.

In spring,
They planted their garden—
but Googie trampled it.

During the summer,
they tended their plants—
and cleaned up litter left by Googie.

When autumn came,
they stored their harvest—
what*ever* Googie hadn't already taken.

Winter arrived,
but Wilbur couldn't sleep.
He was too unhappy.

Wilbur missed clean, peaceful space.
They had to have more space. Lots more space!
He suddenly had a wonderful idea!
Wilbur jumped out of bed, hunted for his tools,

and started to build a SPACE MACHINE.
Wilbur was so excited, he hardly slept all winter.
He planned, measured, whittled, sawed, and drilled.
He pegged, hammered, tacked, tied, and glued—

until finally, in early spring,
his stupendous SPACE MACHINE was finished!

Wilbur started cranking with a fury,
and his machine worked just fine.
There was a great amount of space
billowing out of the nozzle,
just as Wilbur had wanted it to.

But all of that lovely space just went
whooshing back to where it came from!

That wouldn't do at all!

"Wilbur dear, let's put the space into containers
so it can't get away from us," advised Violet.
So—they filled all their boxes,
bottles, jars, pans, and kettles.
Space was crammed into bags, socks, pockets, and pouches.

"What we need are balloons, Violet!" cried Wilbur.
They cranked huge amounts of space
into every balloon that Violet could find.

There was nothing left to fill.
Wilbur was discouraged.
They had great amounts of space—that was true—
but, somehow, they didn't have any room to wiggle!

Wilbur was very tired.
He'd been cranking his machine for months.
Violet squeezed him out the door
and tucked him snugly into the hammock.
"Never mind, dear. You rest for a while,"
she whispered as she kissed him.
"We still have each other."

Wilbur slept, while Violet tried to rearrange
all of the packed-up space in their little house.

The summer sun rose—hot and clear.
Wilbur dreamed he had clean, peaceful space
all around him—
and then he awoke to discover it was not a dream!
"Violet! Look! We have clean, peaceful space again!"

"We certainly do, my dear," sighed Violet
looking at their garden far below,
"and we do still have each other."

"We have each other
AND we have Googie!" moaned Wilbur.

"Oh, dear! His mother will miss him!
What can we do?" asked Violet

"I'll think of something," replied Wilbur.

And he did.